CHEMISTRY

CHEMISTRY

Graham Swift

SHORTLIST

First published in 2008 by
Picador
This Large Print edition published
2012 by AudioGO Ltd
by arrangement with
the Author

ISBN 978 1 4713 1617 3

British Library Cataloguing in Publication Data available

Printed and bound in Great Britain
by MPG Books Group Limited

CONTENTS

Chemistry	1
Learning to Swim	31

CHEMISTRY

The pond in our park was circular, exposed, perhaps fifty yards across. When the wind blew, little waves travelled across it and slapped the paved edges, like a miniature sea. We would go there, Mother, Grandfather and I, to sail the motor-launch Grandfather and I made out of plywood, balsa wood and varnished paper. We would go even in the winter—especially in the winter, because then we would have the pond to ourselves—when the leaves on the two willows turned yellow and dropped and the water froze your hands. Mother would sit on a wooden bench set back from the perimeter; I would prepare the boat for launching. Grandfather, in his black coat and grey scarf, would walk to the far side to receive it. For some reason it was always Grandfather, never I, who went to the far side. When he reached his station I would hear his ‘Ready!’ across the water. A puff of vapour would rise from his lips like the smoke from a muffled pistol. And I would release the launch. It worked by a battery. Its progress was laboured but its course steady. I would watch it head out to the middle while Mother watched behind me. As it moved it seemed that it followed an actual existing line between Grandfather, myself and Mother, as if Grandfather were pulling us towards him on some invisible cord, and that he had to do this to prove we were not beyond his reach. When the boat drew near him he would crouch on his haunches. His hands—which I knew were knotted, veiny and mottled from an accident in one of his chemical experiments—would reach out, grasp it and set it on its return.

The voyages were trouble-free. Grandfather improvised a wire grapnel on the end of a length of fishing line in case of shipwreck or engine failure, but it was never used. Then one day—it must have been soon after Mother met Ralph—we watched the boat, on its first trip across the pond to Grandfather, suddenly become deeper and deeper in the water. The motor cut. The launch wallowed, sank. Grandfather made several throws with his grapnel and pulled out clumps of green slime. I remember what he said to me, on this, the first loss in my life that I had witnessed. He said, very gravely: 'You must accept it—you can't get it back—it's the only way,' as if he were repeating something to himself. And I remember Mother's face as she got up from the bench to leave. It was very still and very white, as if she had seen something appalling.

*   *   *

It was some months after that that Ralph, who was now a regular guest at weekends, shouted over the table to Grandfather: 'Why don't you leave her alone?!'

I remember it because that same Saturday Grandfather recalled the wreck of my boat, and Ralph said to me, as if pouncing on something: 'How about me buying you a new one? How would you like that?' And I said, just to see his face go crestfallen and blank, 'No!', several times, fiercely. Then as we ate supper Ralph suddenly barked, as Grandfather was talking to Mother: 'Why don't you leave her alone?!'

Grandfather looked at him. 'Leave her alone? What do you know about being left alone?' Then he glanced from Ralph to Mother. And Ralph didn't answer, but his face went tight and his hands clenched on his knife and fork.

And all this was because Grandfather had said to Mother: 'You don't make curry any more, the way you did for Alec, the way Vera taught you.'

* * *

It was Grandfather's house we lived in—with Ralph as an ever more permanent lodger. Grandfather and Grandmother had lived in it almost since the day of their marriage. My grandfather had worked for a firm which manufactured gold- and silver-plated articles. My grandmother died suddenly when I was only four, and all I know is that I must have had her looks. My mother said so and so did my father, and Grandfather, without saying anything, would often gaze curiously into my face.

At that time Mother, Father and I lived in a new house some distance from Grandfather's. Grandfather took his wife's death very badly. He needed the company of his daughter and my father, but he refused to leave the house in which my grandmother had lived, and my parents refused to leave theirs. There was bitterness all round, which I scarcely appreciated. Grandfather remained alone in his house, which he ceased to maintain, spending more and more time in his garden shed which he had fitted out for his hobbies of model-making and amateur chemistry.

The situation was resolved in a dreadful way: by my own father's death.

He was required now and then to fly to Dublin or Cork in the light aeroplane belonging to the company he worked for, which imported Irish goods. One day, in unexceptional weather conditions, the aircraft disappeared without trace into the Irish Sea. In a state which resembled a kind of trance—as if some outside force were all the time directing her—my mother sold up our house, put away the money for our joint future, and moved in with Grandfather.

My father's death was a far less remote event than my grandmother's, but no more explicable. I was only seven. Mother said, amidst her adult grief, 'He has gone to where Grandma's gone.' I wondered how Grandmother could be at the bottom of the Irish Sea, and at the same time what Father was doing there. I wanted to know when he would return. Perhaps I knew, even as I asked this, that he never would, that my childish assumptions were only a way of allaying my own grief. But if I really believed Father was gone for ever—I was wrong.

Perhaps too I was endowed with my father's looks no less than my grandmother's. Because when my mother looked at me she would often break into uncontrollable tears and she would clasp me for long periods without letting go, as if afraid I might turn to air.

I don't know if Grandfather took a secret, vengeful delight in my father's death, or if he was capable of it. But fate had made him and his daughter quits and reconciled them in mutual grief. Their situations were equivalent: she a widow and he a widower. And just as my mother could see in me a vestige of my father, so Grandfather could see in the two of us a vestige of my grandmother.

For about a year we lived quietly, calmly, even contentedly within the scope of this sad symmetry. We scarcely made any contact with the outside world. Grandfather still worked, though his retirement age had passed, and would not let Mother work. He kept Mother and me as he might have kept his own wife and son. Even when he did retire we lived quite comfortably on his pension, some savings and a widow's pension my mother got. Grandfather's health showed signs of weakening—he became rheumatic and sometimes short of breath—but he would still go out to the shed in the garden to conduct his chemical experiments, over which he hummed and chuckled gratefully to himself.

We forgot we were three generations. Grandfather bought Mother bracelets and earrings.

Mother called me her 'little man'. We lived for each other—and for those two unfaded memories—and for a whole year, a whole harmonious year, we were really quite happy. Until that day in the park when my boat, setting out across the pond towards Grandfather, sank.

*   *   *

Sometimes when Grandfather provoked Ralph I thought Ralph would be quite capable of jumping to his feet, reaching across the table, seizing Grandfather by the throat and choking him. He was a big man, who ate heartily, and I was often afraid he might hit me. But

Mother somehow kept him in check. Since Ralph's appearance she had grown neglectful of Grandfather. For example—as Grandfather had pointed out that evening—she would cook the things that Ralph liked (rich, thick stews, but not curry) and forget to produce the meals that Grandfather was fond of. But no matter how neglectful and even hurtful she might be to Grandfather herself, she wouldn't have forgiven someone else's hurting him. It would have been the end of her and Ralph. And no matter how much she might hurt Grandfather—to show her allegiance to Ralph—the truth was she really did want to stick by him. She still needed, she couldn't break free of it, that delicate equilibrium that she, he and I had constructed over the months.

I suppose the question was how far Ralph could tolerate not letting go with Grandfather so as to keep Mother, or how far Mother was prepared to turn against Grandfather so as not to lose Ralph. I remember keeping a sort of equation in my head: if Ralph hurts Grandfather it means I'm right—he doesn't really care about Mother at all; but if Mother is cruel to Grandfather (though she would only be cruel to him because she couldn't forsake him) it means she really loves Ralph.

But Ralph only went pale and rigid and stared at Grandfather without moving.

Grandfather picked at his stew. We had already finished ours. He deliberately ate slowly to provoke Ralph.

Then Ralph turned to Mother and said: 'For Christ's sake, we're not waiting all night for him to finish!' Mother blinked and looked frightened. 'Get the pudding!'

You see, he liked his food.

Mother rose slowly and gathered our plates. She looked at me and said, 'Come and help.'

In the kitchen she put down the plates and leaned for several seconds, her back towards me, against the draining board. Then she turned. 'What am I going to do?' She gripped my shoulders. I remembered these were just the words she'd used once before, very soon after Father's death, and then, too, her face had had the same quivery look of being about to spill over. She pulled me towards her. I had a feeling of being back in that old impregnable domain which Ralph had not yet penetrated. Through the window, half visible in the twilight, the evergreen shrubs which filled our garden were defying the onset of autumn. Only the cherry-laurel bushes were partly denuded—for some reason Grandfather had been picking their leaves. I didn't know what to do or say—I should have said something—but inside I was starting to form a plan.

Mother took her hands from

me and straightened up. Her face was composed again. She took the apple crumble from the oven. Burnt sugar and apple juice seethed for a moment on the edge of the dish. She handed me the bowl of custard. We strode, resolutely, back to the table. I thought: now we are going to face Ralph, now we are going to show our solidarity. Then she put down the crumble, began spooning out helpings and said to Grandfather, who was still tackling his stew, 'You're ruining our meal—do you want to take yours out to your shed?!'

*   *   *

Grandfather's shed was more than just a shed. Built of brick in one corner of the high walls surrounding the garden, it was large enough to accommodate a stove, a sink, an old armchair, as well as Grandfather's workbenches and apparatus, and to serve—as it was serving Grandfather more and more—as a miniature home.

I was always wary of entering it. It seemed to me, even before Ralph, even when Grandfather and I constructed the model launch, that it was somewhere where Grandfather went to be alone, undisturbed, to commune perhaps, in some obscure way, with my dead grandmother. But that evening I did not hesitate. I walked along the path by the ivy-clad garden wall. It seemed that his invitation, his loneliness were written in a form only I could read on the dark green door. And when I opened it he said, 'I thought you would come.'

* * *

I don't think Grandfather practised chemistry for any particular reason. He studied it from curiosity and for solace, as some people study the structure of cells under a microscope or watch the changing formation of clouds. In those weeks after Mother drove him out I learnt from Grandfather the fundamentals of chemistry.

I felt safe in his shed. The house where Ralph now lorded it, tucking into bigger and bigger meals, was a menacing place. The shed was another, a sealed-off world. It had a salty, mineral, unhuman smell. Grandfather's flasks, tubes and retort stands would be spread over his workbench. His chemicals were acquired through connections in the metal-plating trade. The stove would be lit in the corner. Beside it would be his meal tray—since, to shame Mother, Grandfather had taken to eating his meals regularly in the shed. A single electric light bulb hung from a beam in the roof. A gas cylinder fed his Bunsen. On one wall was a glass-fronted cupboard in which he grew alum and copper-sulphate crystals.

I would watch Grandfather's experiments. I would ask him to explain what he was doing and to name the contents of his various bottles.

And Grandfather wasn't the same person in his shed as he was in the house—sour and cantankerous. He was a weary, ailing man who winced now and then because of his rheumatism and spoke with quiet self-absorption.

* * *

'What are you making, Grandpa?'

'Not making—changing. Chemistry is the science of change. You don't make things in chemistry—you change them. Anything can change.'

He demonstrated the point by dissolving marble chips in nitric acid. I watched fascinated.

But he went on: 'Anything can change. Even gold can change.'

He poured a little of the nitric acid into a beaker, then took another jar of colourless liquid and added some of its contents to the nitric acid. He stirred the mixture with a glass rod and heated it gently. Some brown fumes came off.

'Hydrochloric acid and nitric acid. Neither would work by itself, but the mixture will.'

Lying on the bench was a pocket watch with a gold chain. I knew it had been given to Grandfather long ago by my grandmother. He unclipped the chain from the watch, then, leaning forward against the bench, he held it between two fingers over the beaker. The chain swung. He eyed me as if he were waiting for me to give some sign. Then he drew the chain away from the beaker.

'You'll have to take my word for it, eh?' He picked up the watch and reattached it to the chain.

'My old job—gold-plating. We used to take real gold and change it. Then we'd take something that wasn't gold at all and cover it with this changed gold so it looked as if it was all gold—but it wasn't.'

He smiled bitterly.

'What are we going to do?'

'Grandpa?'

'People change too, don't they?'

He came close to me. I was barely ten. I looked at him without speaking.

'Don't they?'

He stared fixedly into my eyes, the way I remembered him doing after Grandmother's death.

'They change. But the elements don't change. Do you know what an element is? Gold's an element. We turned it from one form into another, but we didn't make any gold—or lose any.'

Then I had a strange sensation. It seemed to me that Grandfather's face before me was only a cross-section from some infinite stick of rock, from which, at the right point,

Mother's face and mine might also be cut. I thought: every face is like this. I had a sudden giddying feeling that there is no end to anything. I wanted to be told simple, precise facts.

'What's that, Grandpa?'

'Hydrochloric acid.'

'And that?'

'Green vitriol.'

'And that?' I pointed to another, unlabelled jar of clear liquid, which stood at the end of the bench, attached to a complex piece of apparatus.

'Laurel water. Prussic acid.' He smiled. 'Not for drinking.'

* * *

All that autumn was exceptionally cold. The evenings were chill and full of the rustlings of leaves. When I returned to the house from taking out Grandfather's meal tray (this had become my duty) I would observe Mother and Ralph in the living room through the open kitchen hatchway. They would drink a lot from the bottles of whisky and vodka which Ralph brought in and which at first Mother made a show of disapproving. The drink made Mother go soft and heavy and blurred and it made Ralph gain in authority. They would slump together on the sofa. One night I watched Ralph pull Mother towards him and hold her in his arms, his big lurching frame almost enveloping her, and Mother saw me, over Ralph's shoulder, watching from the hatchway. She looked trapped and helpless.

And that was the night that I got my chance—when I went to collect Grandfather's tray. When I entered the shed he was asleep in his chair, his plates, barely touched, on the tray at his feet. In his slumber, his hair dishevelled, mouth open, he looked like some torpid, captive animal that has lost even the will to eat. I had taken an empty spice jar from the kitchen. I took the glass bottle labelled HNO3 and poured some of its contents, carefully, into the spice jar. Then I picked up Grandfather's tray, placed the spice jar beside the plates and carried the tray to the house.

*　　*　　*

I thought I would throw the acid in Ralph's face at breakfast. I didn't want to kill him. It would have been pointless to kill him—since death is a deceptive business. I wanted to spoil his face so Mother would no longer want him. I took the spice jar to my room and hid it in my bedside cupboard. In the morning I would smuggle it down in my trouser pocket. I would wait, pick my moment. Under the table I would remove the stopper. As Ralph gobbled down his eggs and fried bread . . .

I thought I wouldn't be able to sleep. From my bedroom window I could see the dark square of the garden and the little patch of light cast from the window of Grandfather's shed. Often I couldn't sleep until I had seen that patch of light disappear and I knew that Grandfather had shuffled back to the house and slipped in, like a stray cat, at the back door.

But I must have slept that night, since I don't remember seeing Grandfather's light go out or hearing his steps on the garden path.

That night Father came to my bedroom. I knew it was him. His hair and clothes were wet, his lips were caked with salt; seaweed hung from his shoulders. He came and stood by my bed. Where he trod, pools of water formed on the carpet and slowly oozed outwards. For a long time he looked at me. Then he said, 'It was her. She made a hole in the bottom of the boat, not big enough to notice, so it would sink—so you and Grandfather would watch it sink. The boat sank—like my plane.' He gestured to his dripping clothes and encrusted lips. 'Don't you believe me?' He held out a hand to me but I was afraid to take it. 'Don't you believe me? Don't you believe me?' And as he repeated this he walked slowly backwards towards the door, as if something were pulling him, the pools of water at his feet drying instantly. And it was only when he had disappeared that I managed to speak and said: 'Yes. I believe you. I'll prove it.'

And then it was almost light and rain was dashing against the window as if the house were plunging under water and a strange, small voice was calling from the front of the house—but it wasn't Father's voice. I got up, walked out onto the landing and peered through the landing window. The voice was a voice on the radio inside an ambulance which was parked with its doors open by the pavement. The heavy rain and the tossing branches of a rowan tree obscured my view, but I saw the two men in uniform carrying out the stretcher with a blanket draped over it. Ralph was with them. He was wearing his dressing gown and pyjamas and slippers over bare feet, and he carried an umbrella. He fussed around the ambulance men like an overseer directing the loading of some vital piece of cargo. He called something to Mother, who must have been standing below, out of sight at the front door. I ran back across the landing. I wanted to get the acid. But then Mother came up the stairs. She was wearing her dressing gown. She caught me in her arms. I smelt whisky. She said: 'Darling. Please, I'll explain. Darling, darling.'

*   *   *

But she never did explain. All her life since then, I think, she has been trying to explain, or to avoid explaining. She only said: ‘Grandpa was old and ill, he wouldn’t have lived much longer anyway.’ And there was the official verdict: suicide by swallowing prussic acid. But all the other things that should have been explained—or confessed—she never did explain.

And she wore, beneath everything, this look of relief, as if she had recovered from an illness. Only a week after Grandfather’s funeral she went into Grandfather’s bedroom and flung wide the windows. It was a brilliant, crisp late-November day and the leaves on the rowan tree were all gold. And she said: ‘There—isn’t that lovely?’

The day of Grandfather’s funeral had been such a day—hard, dazzling, spangled with early frost and gold leaves. We stood at the ceremony,

Mother, Ralph and I, like a mock version of the trio—Grandfather, Mother and I—who had once stood at my father's memorial service. Mother didn't cry. She hadn't cried at all, even in the days before the funeral when the policemen and the officials from the coroner's court came, writing down their statements, apologizing for their intrusion and asking their questions.

They didn't address their questions to me. Mother said: 'He's only ten, what can he know?' Though there were a thousand things I wanted to tell them—about how Mother banished Grandfather, about how suicide can be murder and how things don't end—which made me feel that I was somehow under suspicion. I took the jar of acid from my bedroom, went to the park and threw it in the pond.

And then after the funeral, after the policemen and officials had gone, Mother and Ralph began to clear out the house and to remove the things from the shed. They tidied the overgrown parts of the garden and clipped back the trees. Ralph wore an old sweater which was far too small for him and I recognized it as one of Father's. And Mother said: 'We're going to move to a new house soon—Ralph's buying it.'

I had nowhere to go. I went down to the park and stood by the pond. Dead willow leaves floated on it. Beneath its surface was a bottle of acid and the wreck of my launch. But though things change they aren't destroyed. It was there, by the pond, when dusk was gathering and it was almost time for the park gates to be locked, as I looked to the centre where my launch sank, then up again to the far side, that I saw him. He was standing in his black overcoat and his grey scarf. The air was very cold and little waves were running across the water. He was smiling, and I knew: the launch was still travelling over to him, unstoppable, unsinkable, along that invisible line. And his hands, his acid-marked hands, would reach out to receive it.

LEARNING TO SWIM

Mrs Singleton had three times thought of leaving her husband. The first time was before they were married, on a charter plane coming back from a holiday in Greece. They were students who had just graduated. They had rucksacks and faded jeans. In Greece they had stayed part of the time by a beach on an island. The island was dry and rocky with great grey- and vermilion-coloured rocks and when you lay on the beach it seemed that you too became a hot, basking rock. Behind the beach there were eucalyptus trees like dry, leafy bones, old men with mules and gold teeth, a fragrance of thyme, and a cafe with melon pips on the floor and a jukebox which played bouzouki music and songs by Cliff Richard. All this Mr Singleton failed to appreciate. He'd only liked the milk-warm, clear-blue sea, in which he'd stayed most of the time as if afraid of foreign soil. On the plane she'd thought: he hadn't enjoyed the holiday, hadn't liked Greece at all. All that sunshine. Then she'd thought she ought not to marry him.

Though she had, a year later.

The second time was about a year after Mr Singleton, who was a civil engineer, had begun his first big job. He became a junior partner in a firm with a growing reputation. She ought to have been pleased by this. It brought money and comfort, it enabled them to move to a house with a large garden, to live well, to think about raising a family. They spent weekends in country hotels. But Mr Singleton seemed untouched by this. He became withdrawn and incommunicative. He went to his work austere-faced. She thought: he likes his bridges and tunnels better than me.

The third time, which was really a phase, not a single moment, was when she began to calculate how often Mr Singleton made love to her. When she started this it was about once every fortnight on average. Then it became every three weeks. The interval had been widening for some time. This was not a predicament Mrs Singleton viewed selfishly. Lovemaking had been a problem before, in their earliest days together, which, thanks to her patience and initiative, had been overcome. It was Mr Singleton's unhappiness, not her own, that she saw in their present plight. He was distrustful of happiness as some people fear heights or open spaces. She would reassure him, encourage him again. But the averages seemed to defy her personal effort: once every three weeks, once every month . . . She thought: things go back to as they were.

But then, by sheer chance, she became pregnant.

Now she lay on her back, eyes

closed, on the coarse sand of the beach in Cornwall. It was hot and, if she opened her eyes, the sky was clear blue. This and the previous summer had been fine enough to make her husband's refusal to go abroad for holidays tolerable. If you kept your eyes closed it could be Greece or Italy or Ibiza. She wore a chocolate-brown bikini, sunglasses, and her skin, which seldom suffered from sunburn, was already beginning to tan. She let her arms trail idly by her side, scooping up little handfuls of sand. If she turned her head to the right and looked towards the sea she could see Mr Singleton and their son Paul standing in the shallow water. Mr Singleton was teaching Paul to swim. 'Kick!' he was saying. From here, against the gentle waves, they looked like no more than two rippling silhouettes.

'Kick!' said Mr Singleton. 'Kick!' He was like a punisher, administering lashes.

She turned her head away to face upwards. If you shut your eyes you could imagine you were the only one on the beach, if you held them shut you could be part of the beach. Mrs Singleton imagined that in order to acquire a tan you had to let the sun make love to you.

She dug her heels in the sand and smiled involuntarily.

When she was a thin, flat-chested, studious girl in a grey school uniform, Mrs Singleton had assuaged her fear and desperation about sex with fantasies which took away from men the brute physicality she expected of them. All her lovers would be artists. Poets would write poems to her, composers would dedicate their works to her. She would even pose, naked and immaculate, for painters, who, having committed her true, her eternal form to canvas, would make love to her in an impalpable, ethereal way, under the power of which her bodily and temporal self would melt away, perhaps for ever. These fantasies (she had never entirely renounced them) had crystallized for her in the image of a sculptor, who from a cold intractable piece of stone would fashion her very essence—which would be vibrant and full of sunlight, like the statues they had seen in Greece.

At university she had worked on the assumption that all men lusted uncontrollably and insatiably after women. She had not yet encountered a man who, while prone to the usual instincts, possessing moreover a magnificent body with which to fulfil them, yet had scruples about doing so, seemed ashamed of his own capacities. It did not matter that Mr Singleton was reading engineering, was scarcely artistic at all, or that his powerful physique was unlike the nebulous creatures of her dreams. She found she loved this solid man-flesh.

Mrs Singleton had thought she was the shy, inexperienced, timid girl. Overnight she discovered that she wasn't this at all. He wore tough denim shirts, spoke and smiled very little and had a way of standing very straight and upright as if he didn't need any help from anyone. She had to educate him into moments of passion, of self-forgetfulness which made her glow with her own achievement. She was happy because she had not thought she was happy and she believed she could make someone else happy. At the university, girls were starting to wear jeans, record-players played the Rolling Stones and in the hush of the Modern Languages Library she read Leopardi and Verlaine. She seemed to float with confidence in a swirling, buoyant element she had never suspected would be her own.

'Kick!' she heard again from the water.

Mr Singleton had twice thought

of leaving his wife. Once was after a symphony concert they had gone to in London when they had not known each other very long and she still tried to get him to read books, to listen to music, to take an interest in art. She would buy concert or theatre tickets, and he had to seem pleased. At this concert a visiting orchestra was playing some titanic, large-scale work by a late-nineteenth-century composer. A note in the programme said it represented the triumph of life over death. He sat on his plush seat amid the swirling barrage of sound. He had no idea what he had to do with it or with the triumph of life over death. He thought the same thought about the rapt girl on his left, the future Mrs Singleton, who now and then bobbed, swayed or rose in her seat as if the music physically lifted her. There were at least seventy musicians on the platform. As the piece worked to its final crescendo the conductor, whose arms were flailing frantically so that his white shirt back appeared under his flying tails, looked so absurd Mr Singleton thought he would laugh. When the music stopped and was immediately supplanted by wild cheering and clapping he thought the world had gone mad. He had struck his own hands together so as to appear to be sharing the ecstasy. Then, as they filed out, he had almost wept because he felt like an insect. He even thought she had arranged the whole business so as to humiliate him.

He thought he would not marry her.

The second time was after they had been married some years. He was one of a team of engineers working on a suspension bridge over an estuary in Ireland. They took it in turns to stay on the site and to inspect the construction work personally. Once he had to go to the very top of one of the two piers of the bridge to examine work on the bearings and housing for the main overhead cables. A lift ran up between the twin towers of the pier amidst a network of scaffolding and power cables to where a working platform was positioned. The engineer, with the supervisor and the foreman, had only to stay on the platform from where all the main features of construction were visible. The men at work on the upper sections of the towers, specialists in their trade, earning up to two hundred pounds a week—who balanced on precarious catwalks and walked along exposed reinforcing girders—often jibed at the engineers who never left the platform. He thought he would show them. He walked out on to one of the catwalks on the outer face of the pier where they were fitting huge grip-bolts. This was quite safe if you held on to the rails but still took some nerve. He wore a check cheesecloth shirt and his white safety helmet. It was a grey, humid August day. The catwalk hung over greyness. The water of the estuary was the colour of dead fish. A dredger was chugging near the base of the pier. He thought: I could swim the estuary, but there is a bridge. Below him the yellow helmets of workers moved over the girders for the roadway like beetles. He took his hands from the rail. He wasn't at all afraid. He had been away from his wife all week. He thought: she knows nothing of this. If he were to step out now into the grey air he would be quite by himself, no harm would come to him . . .

Now Mr Singleton stood in the water, teaching his son to swim. They were doing the water wings exercise. The boy wore a pair of water wings, red underneath, yellow on top, which ballooned up under his arms and chin. With these to support him, he would splutter and splash towards his father who stood facing him some feet away. After a while at this they would try the same procedure, his father moving a little nearer, but without the water wings, and this the boy dreaded. 'Kick!' said Mr Singleton. 'Use your legs!' He watched his son draw painfully towards him. The boy had not yet grasped that the body naturally floated and that if you added to this certain mechanical effects, you swam. He thought that in order to swim you had to make as much frantic movement as possible. As he struggled towards Mr Singleton his head, which was too high out of the water, jerked messily from side to side, and his eyes which were half closed swivelled in every direction but straight ahead. 'Towards me!' shouted Mr Singleton. He held out his arms in front of him for Paul to grasp. As his son was on the point of clutching them he would step back a little, pulling his hands away, in the hope that the last desperate lunge to reach his father might really teach the boy the art of propelling himself in water. But he sometimes wondered if this were his only motive.

'Good boy. Now again.'

At school Mr Singleton had been an excellent swimmer. He had won various school titles, broken numerous records and competed successfully in ASA championships. There was a period between the age of about thirteen and seventeen which he remembered as the happiest in his life. It wasn't the medals and trophies that made him glad, but the knowledge that he didn't have to bother about anything else. Swimming vindicated him. He would get up every morning at six and train for two hours in the baths, and again before lunch. When he fell asleep, exhausted, in French and English periods in the afternoon, he didn't have to bother about the indignation of the masters—lank, ill-conditioned creatures—since he had his excuse. He didn't have to bother about the physics teacher who complained to the headmaster that he would never get the exam results he needed if he didn't cut down his swimming, since the headmaster (who was an advocate of sport) came to his aid and told the physics teacher not to interfere with a boy who was a credit to the school. Nor did he have to bother about a host of other things which were supposed to be going on inside him, which made the question of what to do in the evening, at weekends, fraught and tantalizing, which drove other boys to moodiness and recklessness. Once in the cool water of the baths, his arms reaching, his eyes fixed on the blue marker line on the bottom, his ears full so that he could hear nothing around him, he would feel quite by himself, quite sufficient. At the end of races, when for one brief instant he clung panting alone like a survivor to the finishing rail which his rivals had yet to touch, he felt an infinite peace. He went to bed early, slept soundly, kept to his training regimen; and he enjoyed this Spartan purity which disdained pleasure and disorder. Some of his schoolmates mocked him—for not going to dances on Saturdays or to pubs, under age, or the Expresso after school. But he didn't mind. He didn't need them. He knew they were weak. None of them could hold out, depend on themselves, spurn comfort if they had to. Some of them would go under in life. And none of them could cleave the water as he did or possessed a hard, streamlined, perfectly tuned body like he did.

Then, when he was nearly seventeen, all this changed. His father, who was an engineer, though proud of his son's trophies, suddenly pressed him to different forms of success. The headmaster no longer shielded him from the physics master. He said: 'You can't swim into your future.' Out of spite perhaps or an odd consistency of self-denial, he dropped swimming altogether rather than cut it down. For a year and a half he worked at his maths and physics with the same single-mindedness with which he'd perfected his sport. He knew about mechanics and engineering because he knew how to make his body move through water. His work was not merely competent but good. He got to university, where he might have had the leisure, if he wished, to resume his swimming. But he didn't. Two years are a long gap in a swimmer's training; two years when you are near your peak can mean you will never get back to your true form. Sometimes he went for a dip in the university pool and swam slowly up and down amongst practising members of the university team, whom perhaps he could still have beaten, as a kind of relief.

Often, Mr Singleton dreamt about swimming. He would be moving through vast expanses of water, an ocean. As he moved it did not require any effort at all. Sometimes he would go for long distances under water, but he did not have to bother about breathing. The water would be silvery-grey. And always it seemed that as he swam he was really trying to get beyond the water, to put it behind him, as if it were a veil he were parting and he would emerge on the other side of it at last, on to some pristine shore, where he would step where no one else had stepped before.

When he made love to his wife her body got in the way; he wanted to swim through her.

Mrs Singleton raised herself, pushed her sunglasses up over her dark hair and sat with her arms stretched straight behind her back. A trickle of sweat ran between her breasts. They had developed to a good size since her schoolgirl days. Her skinniness in youth had stood her in good stead against the filling out of middle age, and her body was probably more mellow, more lithe and better proportioned now than it had ever been. She looked at Paul and Mr Singleton half immersed in the shallows. It seemed to her that her husband was the real boy, standing stubbornly upright with his hands before him, and that Paul was some toy being pulled and swung relentlessly around him and towards him as though on some string. They had seen her sit up. Her husband waved, holding the boy's hand, as though for the two of them. Paul did not wave; he seemed more concerned with the water in his eyes. Mrs Singleton did not wave back. She would have done if her son had waved. When they had left for their holiday Mr Singleton had said to Paul, 'You'll learn to swim this time. In salt water, you know, it's easier.' Mrs Singleton hoped her son wouldn't swim; so that she could wrap him, still, in the big yellow towel when he came out, rub him dry and warm, and watch her husband stand apart, his hands empty.

She watched Mr Singleton drop his arm back to his side. 'If you wouldn't splash, it wouldn't go in your eyes,' she just caught him saying.

The night before, in their hotel room, they had argued. They always argued about halfway through their holidays. It was symbolic, perhaps, of that first trip to Greece, when he had somehow refused to enjoy himself. They had to incur injuries so that they could then appreciate their leisure, like convalescents. For the first four days or so of their holiday Mr Singleton would tend to be moody, on edge. He would excuse this as 'winding down', the not-to-be-hurried process of dispelling the pressures of work. Mrs Singleton would be patient. On about the fifth day Mrs Singleton would begin to suspect that the winding down would never end and indeed (which she'd known all along) that it was not winding down at all—he was clinging, as to a defence, to his bridges and tunnels; and she would show her resentment. At this point Mr Singleton would retaliate by an attack upon her indolence.

Last night he had called her 'flabby'. He could not mean, of course, 'flabby-bodied' (she could glance down, now, at her still flat belly), though such a sensual attack would have been simpler, almost heartening, from him. He meant 'flabby of attitude'. And what he meant by this, or what he wanted to mean, was that *he* was not flabby; that he worked, facing the real world, erecting great solid things on the face of the land, and that, while he worked, he disdained work's rewards—money, pleasure, rich food, holidays abroad—that he hadn't 'gone soft', as she'd done since they graduated eleven years ago, with their credentials for the future and their plane tickets to Greece. She knew this toughness of her husband was only a cover for his own failure to relax and his need to keep his distance. She knew that he found no particular virtue in his bridges and tunnels (it was the last thing he wanted to do really—build); it didn't matter if they were right or wrong, they were there, he could point to them as if it vindicated him—just as when he made his infrequent, if seismic love to her it was not a case of enjoyment or satisfaction. He just did it.

It was hot in their hotel room. Mr Singleton stood in his blue pyjama bottoms, feet apart, like a PT instructor.

'Flabby? What do you mean—"flabby"?!' she said, looking daunted.

But Mrs Singleton had the

advantage whenever Mr Singleton accused her in this way of complacency, of weakness. She knew he only did it to hurt her, and so to feel guilty, and so to feel the remorse which would release his own affection for her, his vulnerability, his own need to be loved. Mrs Singleton was used to this process, to the tenderness that was the tenderness of successively opened and reopened wounds. And she was used to being the nurse who took care of the healing scars. For though Mr Singleton inflicted the first blow he would always make himself more guilty than he made her suffer, and Mrs Singleton, though in pain herself, could not resist wanting to clasp and cherish her husband, wanting to wrap him up safe when his own weakness and submissiveness showed and his body became liquid and soft against her; could not resist the old spur that her husband was unhappy and it was for her to make him happy. Mr Singleton was extraordinarily lovable when he was guilty. She would even have yielded indefinitely, foregoing her own grievance, to this extreme of comforting him for the pain he caused her, had she not discovered, in time, that this only pushed the process a stage further. Her forgiveness of him became only another level of comfort, of softness he must reject. His flesh shrank from her restoring touch.

She thought: men go round in circles, women don't move.

She kept to her side of the hotel bed, he, with his face turned, to his. He lay like a person washed up on a beach. She reached out her hand and stroked the nape of his neck. She felt him tense. All this was a pattern.

'I'm sorry,' he said, 'I didn't mean—'

'It's all right, it doesn't matter.'

'Doesn't it matter?' he said.

When they reached this point they

were like miners racing each other for deeper and deeper seams of guilt and recrimination.

But Mrs Singleton had given up delving to rock bottom. Perhaps it was five years ago, when she had thought for the third time of leaving her husband, perhaps long before that. When they were students she'd made allowances for his constraints, his reluctances. An unhappy childhood perhaps, a strict upbringing. She thought his inhibition might be lifted by the sanction of marriage. She'd thought, after all, it would be a good thing if he married her. She had not thought what would be good for her. They stood outside Gatwick Airport, back from Greece, in the grey, wet August light. Their tanned skin had seemed to glow. Yet she'd known this mood of promise would pass. She watched him kick against contentment, against ease, against the long, glittering lifeline she threw to him and, after a while, she ceased to try to haul him in. She began to imagine again her phantom artists. She thought: people slip off the shores of the real world, back into dreams. She hadn't 'gone soft', only gone back to herself. Hidden inside her like treasure there were lines of Verlaine her husband would never appreciate. She thought, he doesn't need me, things run off him, like water. She even thought that her husband's neglect in making love to her was not a problem he had but a deliberate scheme to deny her. When Mrs Singleton desired her husband she could not help herself. She would stretch back on the bed with the sheets pulled off like a blissful nude in a Modigliani. She thought this ought to gladden a man. Mr Singleton would stand at the foot of the bed and gaze down at her. He looked like some strong, chaste knight in the legend of the Grail. He would respond to her invitation, but before he did so there would be this expression, half stern, half innocent, in his eyes. It was the sort of expression that good men in books and films are supposed to make to prostitutes. It would ensure that their lovemaking was marred and that afterwards it would seem as if he had performed something out of duty that only she wanted. Her body would feel like stone. It was at such times, when she felt the cold, deadweight feel of abused happiness, that Mrs Singleton most thought she was through with Mr Singleton. She would watch his strong, compact torso already lifting itself off the bed. She would think: he thinks he is tough, contained in himself, but he won't see what I offer him, he doesn't see how it is I who can help him.

Mrs Singleton lay back on her striped towel on the sand. Once again she became part of the beach. The careless sounds of the seaside, of excited children's voices, of languid grownups', of wooden bats on balls, fluttered over her as she shut her eyes. She thought: it is the sort of day on which someone suddenly shouts, 'Someone is drowning.'

When Mrs Singleton became pregnant she felt she had outmanoeuvred her husband. He did not really want a child (it was the last thing he wanted, Mrs Singleton thought, a child), but he was jealous of her condition, as of some achievement he himself could attain. He was excluded from the little circle of herself and her womb, and, as though to puncture it, he began for the first time to make love to her of a kind where he took the insistent initiative. Mrs Singleton was not greatly pleased. She seemed buoyed up by her own bigness. She noticed that her husband began to do exercises in the morning, in his underpants, press-ups, squat-jumps, as if he were getting in training for something. He was like a boy. He even became, as the term of her pregnancy drew near its end, resilient and detached again, the virile father waiting to receive the son (Mr Singleton knew it would be a son, so did Mrs Singleton) that she, at the appointed time, would deliver him. When the moment arrived he insisted on being present so as to prove he wasn't squeamish and to make sure he wouldn't be tricked in the transaction. Mrs Singleton was not daunted. When the pains became frequent she wasn't at all afraid. There were big watery lights clawing down from the ceiling of the delivery room like the lights in dentists' surgeries. She could just see her husband looking down at her. His face was white and clammy. It was his fault for wanting to be there. She had to push, as though away from him. Then she knew it was happening. She stretched back. She was a great surface of warm, splitting rock and Paul was struggling bravely up into the sunlight. She had to coax him with her cries. She felt him emerge like a trapped survivor. The doctor groped with rubber gloves. 'There we are,' he said. She managed to look at Mr Singleton. She wanted suddenly to put him back inside for good where Paul had come from. With a fleeting pity she saw that this was what Mr Singleton wanted too. His eyes were half closed. She kept hers on him. He seemed to wilt under her gaze. All his toughness and control were draining from him and she was glad. She lay back triumphant and glad. The doctor was holding Paul, but she looked, beyond, at Mr Singleton. He was far away like an insect. She knew he couldn't hold out. He was going to faint. He was looking where her legs were spread. His eyes went out of focus. He was going to faint, keel over, right there on the spot.

Mrs Singleton grew restless,

though she lay unmoving on the beach. Wasps were buzzing close to her head, round their picnic bag. She thought that Mr Singleton and Paul had been too long at their swimming lesson. They should come out. It never struck her, hot as she was, to get up and join her husband and son in the sea. Whenever Mrs Singleton wanted a swim she would wait until there was an opportunity to go in by herself; then she would wade out, dip her shoulders under suddenly and paddle about contentedly, keeping her hair dry, as though she were soaking herself in a large bath. They did not bathe as a family; nor did Mrs Singleton swim with Mr Singleton—who now and then, too, would get up by himself and enter the sea, swim at once about fifty yards out, then cruise for long stretches, with a powerful crawl or butterfly, back and forth across the bay. When this happened Mrs Singleton would engage her son in talk so he would not watch his father. Mrs Singleton did not swim with Paul either. He was too old, now, to cradle between her knees in the very shallow water, and she was somehow afraid that while Paul splashed and kicked around her he would suddenly learn how to swim. She had this feeling that Paul would only swim while she was in the sea, too. She did not want this to happen, but it reassured her and gave her sufficient confidence to let Mr Singleton continue his swimming lessons with Paul. These lessons were obsessive, indefatigable. Every Sunday morning at seven, when they were at home, Mr Singleton would take Paul to the baths for yet another attempt. Part of this, of course, was that Mr Singleton was determined that his son should swim, but it enabled him also to avoid the Sunday morning languor: extra hours in bed, leisurely lovemaking.

Once, in a room at college, Mr

Singleton had told Mrs Singleton about his swimming, about his training sessions, races; about what it felt like when you could swim really well. She had run her fingers over his long naked back.

Mrs Singleton sat up and rubbed suntan lotion onto her thighs. Down near the water's edge, Mr Singleton was standing about waist deep, supporting Paul, who, gripped by his father's hands, water wings still on, was flailing, face down, at the surface. Mr Singleton kept saying, 'No, keep still.' He was trying to get Paul to hold his body straight and relaxed so he would float. But each time as Paul nearly succeeded he would panic, fearing his father would let go, and thrash wildly. When he calmed down and Mr Singleton held him, Mrs Singleton could see the water running off his face like tears.

Mrs Singleton did not alarm herself at this distress of her son. It was a guarantee against Mr

Singleton's influence, an assurance that Paul was not going to swim; nor was he to be imbued with any of his father's sullen hardiness. When Mrs Singleton saw her son suffer, it pleased her and she felt loving towards him. She felt that an invisible thread ran between her and the boy which commanded him not to swim, and she felt that Mr Singleton knew that it was because of her that his efforts with Paul were in vain. Even now, as Mr Singleton prepared for another attempt, the boy was looking at her smoothing the suntan oil onto her legs.

'Come on, Paul,' said Mr Singleton. His wet shoulders shone like metal.

When Paul was born it seemed to Mrs Singleton that her life with her husband was dissolved, as a mirage dissolves, and that she could return again to what she was before she knew him. She let her staved-off hunger for happiness and her old suppressed dreams revive. But then they were not dreams, because they had a physical object and she knew she needed them in order to live. She did not disguise from herself what she needed. She knew that she wanted the kind of close, even erotic relationship with her son that women who have rejected their husbands have been known to have. The kind of relationship in which the son must hurt the mother, the mother the son. But she willed it, as if there would be no pain. Mrs Singleton waited for her son to grow. She trembled when she thought of him at eighteen or twenty. When he was grown he would be slim and light and slender, like a boy even though he was a man. He would not need a strong body because all his power would be inside. He would be all fire and life in essence. He would become an artist, a sculptor. She would pose for him naked (she would keep her body trim for this), and he would sculpt her. He would hold the chisel. His hands would guide the cold metal over the stone and its blows would strike sunlight.

Mrs Singleton thought: all the best statues they had seen in Greece seemed to have been dredged up from the sea.

She finished rubbing the lotion onto her insteps and put the cap back on the tube. As she did so she heard something that made her truly alarmed. It was Mr Singleton saying, 'That's it, that's the way! At last! Now keep it going!' She looked up. Paul was in the same position as before but he had learnt to make slower, regular motions with his limbs and his body no longer sagged in the middle. Though he still wore the water wings he was moving, somewhat laboriously, forwards so that Mr Singleton had to walk along with him, and at one point Mr Singleton removed one of his hands from under the boy's ribs and simultaneously looked at his wife and smiled. His shoulders flashed. It was not a smile meant for her. She could see that. And it was not one of her husband's usual, infrequent, rather mechanical smiles. It was the smile a person makes about some joy inside, hidden and incommunicable.

That's enough, thought Mrs Singleton, getting to her feet, pretending not to have noticed, behind her sunglasses, what had happened in the water. It *was* enough: they had been in the water for what seemed like an hour. He was only doing it because of their row last night, to make her feel he was not outmatched by using the reserve weapon of Paul. And, she added with relief to herself, Paul still had the water wings and one hand to support him.

'That's enough now!' she shouted aloud, as if she were slightly, but not ill-humouredly, peeved at being neglected. ‘Come on in now!’ She had picked up her purse as a quickly conceived ruse as she got up and as she walked towards the water’s edge she waved it above her head. ‘Who wants an ice cream?’

Mr Singleton ignored his wife. ‘Well done, Paul,’ he said. ‘Let’s try that again.’

Mrs Singleton knew he would do this. She stood on the little ridge of sand just above where the beach, becoming fine shingle, shelved into the sea. She replaced a loose strap of her bikini over her shoulder and with a finger of each hand pulled the bottom half down over her buttocks. She stood feet apart, slightly on her toes, like a gymnast. She knew other eyes on the beach would be on her. It flattered her that she—and her husband, too—received admiring glances from those around. She thought, with relish for the irony: perhaps they think we are happy, beautiful people. For all her girlhood diffidence, Mrs Singleton enjoyed displaying her attractions, and she liked to see other people's pleasure. When she lay sunbathing she imagined making love to all the moody, pubescent boys on holiday with their parents, with their slim waists and their quick heels.

'See if you can do it without me holding you,' said Mr Singleton. 'I'll help you at first.' He stooped over Paul. He looked like a mechanic making final adjustments to some prototype machine.

'Don't you want an ice cream, then, Paul?' said Mrs Singleton. 'They've got those chocolate ones.'

Paul looked up. His short wet hair stood up in spikes. He looked like a prisoner offered a chance of escape, but the plastic water wings, like some absurd pillory, kept him fixed.

Mrs Singleton thought: he crawled out of me, now I have to lure him back with ice cream.

'Can't you see he was getting the

hang of it?' Mr Singleton said. 'If he comes out now he'll—'

'Hang of it! It was you. You were holding him all the time.'

She thought: perhaps I am hurting my son.

Mr Singleton glared at Mrs Singleton. He gripped Paul's shoulders. 'You don't want to get out now, do you, Paul?' He looked suddenly as if he really might drown Paul rather than let him come out.

Mrs Singleton's heart raced. She wasn't good at rescues, at resuscitations. She knew this because of her life with her husband.

'Come on, you can go back in later,' she said.

Paul was a hostage. She was playing for time, not wanting to harm the innocent.

She stood on the sand like a marooned woman watching for ships. The sea, in the sheltered bay, was almost flat calm. A few glassy waves idled in but were smoothed out before they could break. On the headlands there were outcrops of scaly rocks like basking lizards. The island in Greece had been where Theseus left Ariadne. Out over the blue water, beyond the heads of bobbing swimmers, seagulls flapped like scraps of paper.

Mr Singleton looked at Mrs Singleton. She was a fussy mother daubed with Ambre Solaire, trying to bribe her son with silly ice creams; though if you forgot this she was a beautiful, tanned girl, like the girls men imagine on desert islands. But then, in Mr Singleton's dreams, there was no one else on the untouched shore he ceaselessly swam to.

He thought, if Paul could swim, then I could leave her.

Mrs Singleton looked at her husband. She felt afraid. The water's edge was like a dividing line between them which marked off the territory in which each existed. Perhaps they could never cross over.

‘Well, I’m getting the ice creams. You’d better get out.’

She turned and paced up the sand. Behind the beach was an ice-cream van painted like a fairground.

Paul Singleton looked at his mother. He thought: she is deserting me—or I am deserting her. He wanted to get out to follow her. Her feet made puffs of sand which stuck to her ankles, and you could see all her body as she strode up the beach. But he was afraid of his father and his gripping hands. And he was afraid of his mother, too. How she would wrap him, if he came out, in the big yellow towel like egg yolk, how she would want him to get close to her smooth, sticky body, like a mouth that would swallow him. He thought: the yellow towel humiliated him, his father’s hands humiliated him. The water wings humiliated him: you put them on and became a puppet. So much of life is humiliation. It was how you won love.

His father was taking off the water wings like a man unlocking a chastity belt. He said: 'Now try the same, coming towards me.' His father stood some feet away from him. He was a huge, straight man, like the pier of a bridge. 'Try.' Paul Singleton was six. He was terrified of water. Every time he entered it he had to fight down fear. His father never realized this. He thought it was simple, you said, 'Only water, no need to be afraid.' His father did not know what fear was; the same as he did not know what fun was. Paul Singleton hated water. He hated it in his mouth and in his eyes. He hated the chlorine smell of the swimming baths, the wet, slippery tiles, the echoing whoops and screams. He hated it when his father read to him from *The Water Babies*. It was the only story his father read, because, since he didn't know fear or fun, he was really sentimental. His mother read lots of stories.

'Come on, then. I'll catch you.' Paul Singleton held out his arms and raised one leg. This was the worst moment. Perhaps having no help was most humiliating. If you didn't swim you sank like a statue. They would drag him out, his skin streaming. His father would say: 'I didn't mean . . .' But if he swam, his mother would be forsaken. She would stand on the beach with chocolate ice cream running down her arm. There was no way out, there were all these things to be afraid of and no weapons. But then, perhaps he was not afraid of his mother nor his father, nor of water, but of something else. He had felt it just now—when he'd struck out with rhythmic, reaching strokes and his feet had come off the bottom and his father's hand had slipped from under his chest: as if he had mistaken what his fear was, as if he had been unconsciously pretending, even to himself, so as to execute some plan.

He lowered his chin into the water. 'Come on!' said Mr Singleton. He launched himself forward and felt the sand leave his feet and his legs wriggle like cut ropes. 'There,' said his father as he realized. 'There!' His father stood like a man waiting to clasp a lover, there was a gleam on his face. 'Towards me! Towards me!' said his father suddenly. But he kicked and struck, half in panic, half in pride, away from his father, away from the shore, away, in this strange new element that seemed all his own.

Checkout Receipt

Ardkeen Library 051-849755
12/06/15 12:45

For renewal/enquiries phone 051- 849755

PATRON: Kelly Nan

Healing foods /
ANF
CALL NO: 641.5631
30005002477746 23/06/15

Red sky in morning /
LPF
CALL NO: LYN
30005004633551 23/06/15

Chemistry [text (large print)] /
ALF
CALL NO: SWI
30005004546845 03/07/15

The thief /
ALF
CALL NO: REN
30005004940089 03/07/15

Departures [text (large print)] /
ALF
CALL NO: PAR
30005004546779 03/07/15

TOTAL: 5